Margaret Miller

NOW I'M BIG

Greenwillow Books, New York

The full-color photographs were reproduced from 35-mm
Kodachrome slides. The text type is Swiss 721 BT.

First Edition   10 9 8 7 6 5 4 3 2 1

Library of Congress Cataloging-in-Publication Data

Miller, Margaret (date)
Now I'm big / by Margaret Miller.
        p.   cm.
Summary: Several children reflect on the things they did as
babies as opposed to the things they are able to do now that
they are a little older and bigger.
ISBN 0-688-14077-7 (trade).   ISBN 0-688-14078-5 (lib. bdg.)
[1. Babies—Fiction.   2. Growth—Fiction.   3. Size—Fiction.]
I. Title.   PZ7.M628No   1996   [E]—dc20   95-17774
CIP   AC

For Jacob,
who used to be little . . .

Many thanks to everyone—big and little—who appears in this book: Michael Beraka; Miranda Berman; Jonah Bleckner; Sarabeth Boak; Lyn, Wesley, and Madison Edens; Timmy Ford; Olivia Jae Fass; Arielle Green; Max Greenberg; Hanna Bille Harding; Hailey McInerney; Chloe, Hermia, and Stephen Nelson; Andrew Roberts; Sydney Schmerzler; Craig Anthony Simmons, Jr.; Simone Teitelbaum; Sybil Weise; and Christopher, Jillian, and Janice Williams.

When we were born
we were very small.

Now we're big!

When I was a baby

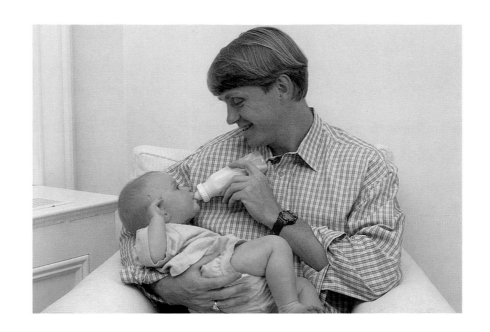

I got milk from a bottle
and I slept in a crib.

Now I'm big!

  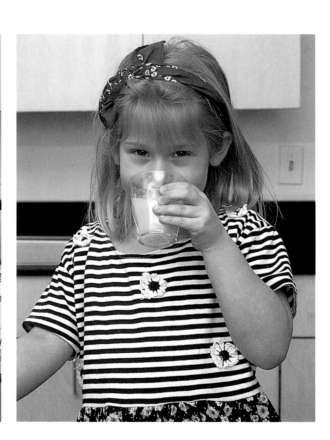

I drink juice in a glass

and I sleep in my bed.

When I was little

I made lots of messes and my mom had to wash me.

Now I'm big!

Sometimes my hands get messy

but I clean myself up.

When I was a baby

I had a favorite stuffed animal
and I played with blocks.

Now I'm big!

I take care of a real dog

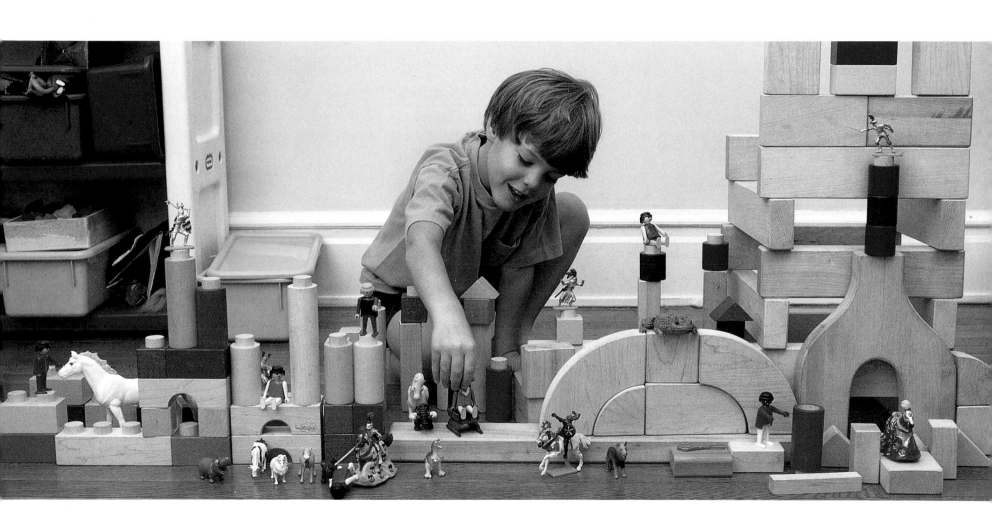

and I'm still playing with blocks, but it's different.

When I was little

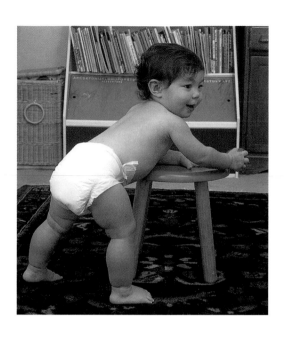

**I wore diapers and
my parents dressed me.**

Now I'm big!

I wear underwear,

I choose my own clothes,

**and
I dress
myself.**

Molly

When I was a baby

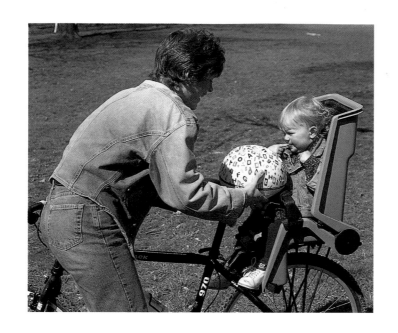

**I rode on my mom's bike
and I rocked on a wooden horse.**

Now I'm big!

I pedal my own bicycle

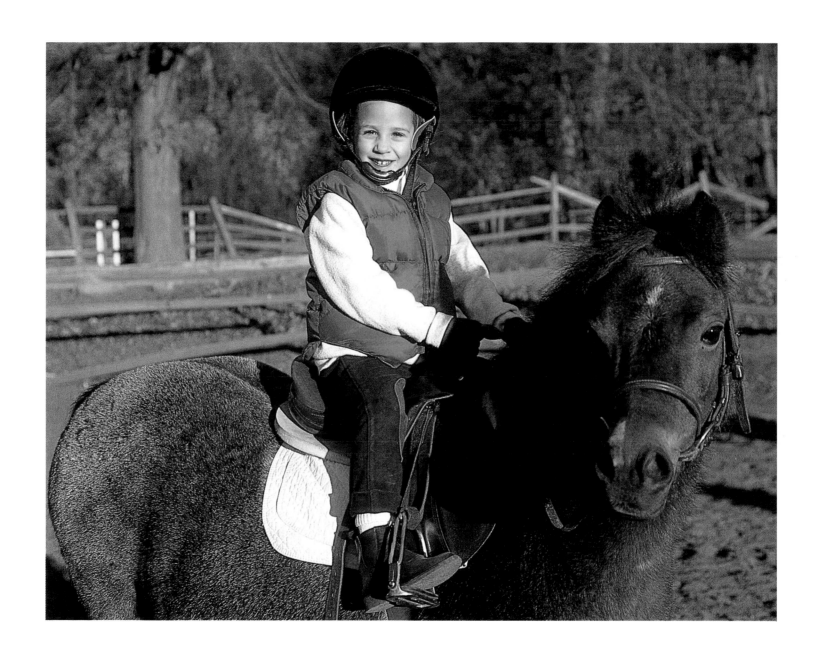

and I ride a brown pony.

When I was little

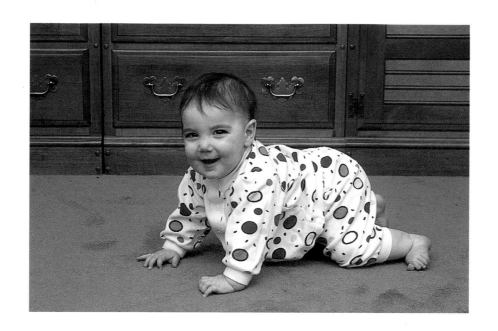

I crawled on my hands and knees and I played by myself.

Now I'm big!

I can climb and jump

and I play games with my friends.

We used to be little,
and now we're big.
Look how we've grown!

MARGARET MILLER is a freelance photographer who lives in New York City with her husband, two children, and two dogs. She traces her love of photography to her childhood. "My mother is a wonderful photographer and I grew up in a house filled with family photographs. I especially loved being with her in the darkroom. I also spent many hours looking through two very powerful books, *The Family of Man* edited by Edward Steichen, and *You Have Seen Their Faces* by Erskine Caldwell and Margaret Bourke-White. After college I worked in children's book publishing for a number of years. I had always taken photographs of my family and I was fortunate in realizing my goal of combining my two long-time interests—photography and children's books."

Margaret Miller is the author/photographer of *Whose Hat?*; *Who Uses This?*; *Where Does It Go?*, a *New York Times* Best Illustrated Book of 1992; *Can You Guess?*; *My Five Senses*; and *Where's Jenna?* She is also the photographer for *Ramona: Behind the Scenes of a Television Show*; *Adventure in Space: The Flight to Fix the Hubble*; *Your New Potty*; *My Puppy Is Born*; *How You Were Born*; *My New Kitten*; and *Riding Silver Star*.